Elaine Booth

# LUCY DANIELS

# Pets'
# Party

### Illustrated by Paul Howard

*Hodder*
*Children's*
*Books*

a division of Hodder Headline plc

**Special thanks to Helen Magee**

Text copyright © 1998  Ben M. Baglio
Created by Ben M. Baglio, London W12 7QY
Illustrations copyright © 1998 Paul Howard
Cover illustration by Chris Chapman

First published in Great Britain in 1998
by Hodder Children's Books

A Catalogue record for this book is available from the British Library

ISBN 0 340 73605 4

Typeset by Avon Dataset Ltd, Bidford-on-Avon, Warks

Printed and bound in Great Britain by
The Guernsey Press Co. Ltd., Guernsey, Channel Islands

Hodder Children's Books
a division of Hodder Headline plc
338 Euston Road
London NW1 3BH

# Contents

*To Joseph Jack*

# 1

# *A new boy at school*

"Come on, James, the bell's gone." Mandy Hope shivered as she called over her shoulder to her best friend. She could feel her cheeks glowing red. The wind was blowing cold off the moors that surrounded the village of Welford. Mandy was glad of the bright woolly scarf Gran had knitted for her. It kept her cosy even in the chilliest of winds.

*It's nearly Christmas*, Mandy thought happily. Maybe there would be snow soon. James Hunter ran through the school gate behind her. As he went, he skidded on a patch of ice and bumped into a thin, elderly lady. She was muffled up in a long black coat and had a black felt hat pulled down over her ears.

"Sorry, Mrs Trigg," James apologised.

Mrs Trigg gave James a severe look. "Really, James, why weren't you looking where you were going?" she asked sternly.

"I slipped on some ice," James protested.

"You shouldn't have been running," Mrs Trigg replied. "You children are always running everywhere. Max is just the same."

*Max*, Mandy thought. *Mrs Trigg's grandson*. Mrs Trigg lived in Holly Cottage, near to Lilac Cottage where Mandy's gran and grandad lived. Mandy's gran had told her that Max was coming to stay with his gran until after Christmas, because his dad was working away and his mum had gone into hospital.

"Hello, Mrs Trigg," Mandy said. "Has

your grandson arrived yet?"

"I've just left him with his teacher," Mrs Trigg replied. "He's going to be in Mrs Todd's class."

Mandy nodded. "Mrs Todd is my teacher too," she said. "I'll look after Max if you like. James and I can introduce him to *everybody*!"

Mrs Trigg smiled. "That would be very kind, Mandy," she said. "I thought it would do him good to spend the week before the Christmas holidays at school with all the other children. *I* won't be much company for him."

Mandy smiled back, pleased. Mrs Trigg hardly ever smiled; she usually looked worried. Mandy thought she seemed much nicer when she smiled.

"It'll be lovely for you having Max to stay, won't it?" Mandy said. "I'm sure he'll enjoy it too."

"I hope so," Mrs Trigg replied. Then she sighed. "It's that dog of his that really worries me. It's going to be such trouble."

"Dog!" Mandy exclaimed. "He's brought a dog with him?" Mandy loved animals, which was just as well, as her parents were vets in Welford. They lived in Animal Ark, a stone-built cottage with a surgery attached. Mandy loved meeting all her parents' animal patients.

"I've told Max the dog has to sleep in the potting shed," Mrs Trigg went on. "I don't want all the mess and bother that pets make."

Mandy bit back her reply. Because Animal Ark was so busy with animal patients,

Mandy wasn't allowed a pet for the time being, though she would have loved one. She couldn't imagine a pet ever being a bother.

"Come on, Mandy," James urged her. "The bell went ages ago."

Mandy waved goodbye to Mrs Trigg and raced into school. She couldn't wait to meet Max's dog. A cold gust of wind blew as she crossed the school yard. She shivered and pulled her soft, red scarf up to her chin. Imagine making a dog sleep in the potting shed in this weather. Poor thing!

"What's your dog's name?" Mandy asked Max at morning playtime.

Everyone had crowded round Max, telling him all about Welford and trying to make him welcome.

"Sandy," Max replied. "He's a Cairn terrier. My dad gave him to me before he went to work abroad. He's six months old now."

"So he's still a puppy!" Mandy exclaimed delightedly.

"Peter's got a Cairn, too. He's called Timmy," James told Max.

"But Timmy's more of a *terror* than a *terrier*," Peter Foster added, grinning. "He's the naughtiest dog in Welford."

Max's big blue eyes lit up. "Cairns aren't really naughty," he said. "They've just got lots of energy. Maybe Sandy and Timmy could be friends."

"And James has a Labrador. His name is Blackie," Mandy told Max. "Blackie *loves* making friends with other dogs."

"I bet Blackie doesn't have to sleep in the potting shed," Max said.

"Of course he doesn't," James replied fiercely. Then he looked sympathetically at Max. "Your gran told us that Sandy had to. Won't she let him into the house at all?"

Max shook his head. His eyes looked sad. "She thinks he would make too much mess."

Mandy felt very sorry for Max. "Why don't you bring Sandy round to Animal Ark?" she suggested. "And we can take him and Blackie out for walks. Blackie would love that, wouldn't he, James?"

James nodded. "And you can bring him carol singing the day before Christmas Eve," he added. "There will be loads of us going round the village, and everyone is going to bring their pets."

"I won't be able to bring Toto though," Jill Redfern said. "Toto is a tortoise and tortoises hibernate in winter."

"But I'm bringing Duchess, my Persian cat," said Richard Tanner.

"And I'm bringing Minnie, my mouse," Amy Fenton piped up. "Of course, I'll have to wrap her up warmly."

Mandy smiled and looked up at the sky. "Do you think there will be snow for Christmas?" she asked.

"I hope so," Max said. "At least then it will seem a bit more *like* Christmas." Then his face fell. "But then it might be too cold for Sandy in the potting shed."

Mandy looked at him in concern. "You aren't unhappy at Holly Cottage, are you?" she asked.

Max looked at the floor, then back at

Mandy. "Not really," he said. "I love my gran but it isn't like being at home. Mum and Dad don't mind if Sandy jumps on the furniture or anything, but Gran is so fussy about things like that. And she doesn't even have a Christmas tree. Mum and Dad and I decorate a Christmas tree every year and now I won't be with them for Christmas. Dad is working abroad and he isn't sure if he'll be able to get home for Christmas. And now Mum might not be home, either." Max looked even more sad.

"I'll tell you what," Mandy suggested.

"James and I are going round to *my* gran's after school for tea. She lives at Lilac Cottage, just down from your gran's. Why don't we bring Blackie to meet Sandy afterwards?"

"Would you?" asked Max. "I'd really like that – and so would Sandy."

"It's a date," said Mandy. "And, I promise you, Max, you're going to have a great Christmas in Welford. We'll make sure of it; won't we, everybody?" Mandy looked round at her friends. They all nodded in agreement.

"Of course we will," Gary Roberts said. "You can come and see Gertie, my garter-snake, if you like."

"How would you like to have a ride on Paddy, my pony?" Paul Stevens asked.

Max laughed. "I'd love it," he replied. "Is Welford full of animals?"

"Just wait till you see Animal Ark," Mandy told him. "At the moment we've got a parrot and a rabbit, two kittens and a gerbil, a hamster, a budgie and three guinea-pigs."

"Wow!" said Max. "You're going to have a full house for Christmas."

Mandy shook her head. "Mum and Dad like to send as many animals as possible home at Christmas," she explained. "They're working really hard to get them all well enough to go back to their owners by Christmas Eve."

"I'll have to hurry if I want to see all the animals before they leave, then," said Max. "Can I really come to Animal Ark?"

"So long as you promise to bring Sandy," Mandy insisted.

"That's no problem," Max replied, smiling. "Sandy and I go everywhere together."

The bell rang for the end of playtime and Mandy looked across at James. He gave her the thumbs-up sign. If it was up to Welford Village Primary School, Max was going to have a very good Christmas indeed! But one thing still troubled Mandy. Sandy's Christmas would be no fun at all if Mrs Trigg had anything to do with it. Mandy couldn't bear the thought of the poor puppy

out in the cold potting shed on his own.
She frowned. Somehow she had to change
Mrs Trigg's mind!

# 2
# *Meeting Sandy*

"Just imagine it, Gran!" Mandy wailed when she and James were at Lilac Cottage, having tea. "Sandy has to sleep in the potting shed!"

"Now, now, Mandy," Grandad put in. "I'm sure Maggie Trigg has got a snug, warm bed made up for the little fellow. She's a kind woman. She would never be cruel to an animal."

"She's just very house-proud," Gran said, putting a plate of cheese sandwiches, and another one of home-made ginger cake, on the table.

James slipped a bit of cheese sandwich to Blackie. The Labrador pup gobbled it up and thumped his tail on the floor. At least *Blackie* was happy!

Mandy sighed. "Why doesn't Mrs Trigg like animals, Gran?"

Gran shrugged. "I don't think Maggie dislikes animals," she replied. "I would imagine that she just thinks they make a lot of mess. You know, she used to be a rather jolly, happy-go-lucky sort of person. She used to enjoy coming to the Women's Institute with me."

"And she used to be very involved in Welford's amateur dramatic society," Grandad added.

"Mrs Trigg?" exclaimed Mandy.

Grandad nodded. "Maggie and her husband, Bill, directed the Christmas panto every year in the church hall," he went on. "But a few years ago Bill died, and since then Maggie seems to have lost interest in everything, poor woman."

"She doesn't get involved with anything any more," Gran agreed. "She spends all her time cleaning her house. It's as if she decided to put all her love and care into Holly Cottage."

"I think it will be good for Maggie to have Max staying with her," Grandad said thoughtfully. "It'll give her someone else to care for."

"You could be right, Tom," Mandy's gran replied. "I think she's lonely."

"So why doesn't she get a pet?" Mandy asked, helping herself to a large piece of ginger cake. "No, don't tell me – it would make too much mess." She sighed again. "Do you think Mrs Trigg will ever change her mind about animals?"

Grandad ruffled Mandy's short fair hair. "Are you going to make a project out of Maggie Trigg?" he asked, his eyes twinkling.

Mandy stopped chewing for a moment. "Maybe I will," she said. "Maybe that's *just* what I'll do."

James shoved his glasses up on his nose and rolled his eyes. "Uh-oh," he said. "Poor Mrs Trigg."

"Poor Sandy!" Mandy retorted. Then she smiled. "Let's go! I can't wait to meet him!"

Mandy and James raced a few houses down the lane to Holly Cottage. Blackie bounded along beside them, enjoying the run.

"There's somebody in the potting shed," James said, as they went through the gate.

Warm yellow light spilled out of the window of the potting shed on to the path. The winter afternoon was growing dark and the little shed looked cosy.

Max popped his head round the potting shed door as he heard their voices. "In here," he said. "Sandy is waiting for you."

Mandy ran towards the shed door and a furry bundle launched itself at her. "Oh, aren't you gorgeous!" she exclaimed as Sandy jumped up and put his two front paws on her legs. "I can see why you call him Sandy, Max."

The little terrier was a pale golden colour.

His shaggy coat looked thick and well groomed. Max obviously took very good care of his pet. Mandy bent down and fussed over Sandy, rubbing his ears. The puppy rolled over on to his back and she tickled his tummy.

Blackie scampered into the shed after James. The Labrador wagged his tail furiously when he saw Sandy.

"Hey, watch out!" Max said, grabbing a packet of seeds that Blackie's tail had knocked off a low shelf.

Blackie took no notice. He was already

snuffling at Sandy's nose, butting the other pup playfully. Sandy sprang up and butted Blackie back. Soon the two dogs were rolling on the potting shed floor, playing and getting to know each other.

James laughed. "I reckon they're friends already," he remarked.

Max looked proudly at his pet. "Sandy just loves company," he said. "I hate leaving him in here on his own."

Mandy looked round the shed. There was a dog basket in one corner with a warm, woolly blanket inside. Beside it was a food bowl, a water bowl and a hot-water bottle.

"I put the hot-water bottle there in case he gets cold during the night," Max told them.

Mandy looked at Max sympathetically. "You've made the shed really comfortable for him," she said. "I'm sure he'll be all right. Cairn terriers have lovely thick, warm coats."

Max's mouth drooped. "It's just that I'm so used to having him around," he explained. "What if he misses me during the night? He'll howl his head off. And what about during the day when I'm at school? Who's going to take him for a walk? He'll probably cry all day."

James frowned. "Your gran won't like that," he said.

"Max!" called a voice from the back door of the cottage. "Max, where are you?"

"In the potting shed, Gran," Max called back. "Mandy and James have come to visit Sandy."

Mrs Trigg peered out from the kitchen door. "It's cold out there," she said. "Come inside." The old lady turned and went back into the house.

Blackie sat up, his ears pricked. Before James could stop him, the Labrador had galloped up the path and into the cottage.

"Uh-oh," said James. "Blackie, come back!"

Sandy gave a short bark and raced up the path after Blackie.

"Sandy!" Max shouted. But both dogs had disappeared.

Mandy, James and Max all dived out

through the door of the shed, hurtling up the path after the dogs. Mandy got to the kitchen door first, and winced as she heard a dreadful clatter.

Mrs Trigg was standing in the middle of the kitchen, looking very annoyed. A pot stand had been overturned and the floor was littered with pots and pan. "*Now* do you see why I don't let dogs in the house, Max?" Mrs Trigg said, as he came into the kitchen with James. "Look what those dogs have done. I'm beginning to think it would be better to send Sandy to kennels if he's going to behave like this."

Max gasped. "Oh, no, Gran!" he pleaded, as he bent to pick up the pots and pans. "Sandy didn't mean any harm. I'll clear this up. Please don't send him away."

Mrs Trigg looked at Max's white, worried face, and her own stern expression softened just a little. "Now, now," she said. "There's no need to get so upset over an animal, Max."

"But he isn't just an animal," Max protested. "He's *Sandy*. Dad gave him to me before he went to work abroad, and I promised Mum I would take good care of him while she was in hospital. I'm all he's got just now!" Mandy could see that he was holding back his tears.

Mrs Trigg looked shocked at Max's outburst. "Oh dear," she sighed, ruffling her grandson's hair. "You're missing your mum and dad a lot, aren't you?" She didn't seem angry any more.

Max nodded. "Do you think maybe Mum will be out of hospital for Christmas?" he asked.

"I'm afraid not, Max," she said softly. "I rang the hospital today and they don't think that's very likely."

Max hung his head and Sandy reached up to him, licking his hand. "Oh, Sandy," Max said, burying his face in Sandy's neck.

Mrs Trigg's expression softened as she looked at Max and Sandy. "Don't worry about the kennels, Max," she said. "We'll manage somehow."

"You mean you won't send him away?" Max asked, hopefully.

Mrs Trigg sighed and set the pot stand upright. "Not if he behaves himself," she said at last, looking down at the puppy. Sandy put his head on one side and looked appealingly up at Mrs Trigg. "Bad dog!" she said to him. But Mandy noticed the old lady couldn't help smiling a little as she helped Max replace the pots and pans.

Sandy scampered over to Mrs Trigg and began trying to undo her shoe laces, wagging his stumpy tail. He put a paw on top of her left foot and rubbed his head against her ankle. Mandy was pleased to see that Mrs

Trigg didn't push the puppy away.

Max scooped him up. "I'll take him back to the potting shed," he said. "He'll be good, I promise, Gran."

Mrs Trigg shook her head. "Come near the fire and get warm first. You can take him out later. Leave him in here in the kitchen for now. Come on, all of you."

James looked at Mandy as Mrs Trigg led the way out of the kitchen. "Where's Blackie?" he mouthed.

Mandy gasped. "I'd forgotten about Blackie," she confessed. "Where on earth has he got to?"

# 3

# *Pets in trouble!*

Mrs Trigg's voice floated back to them from the living-room. "Well, of all the cheek!" she exclaimed.

Mandy and James hurried into the living-room behind her. "Oh, no!" said James.

Blackie was stretched out on the sofa in front of the fire. His eyes were closed and he was snoozing peacefully. An embarrassed

James collared Blackie and dragged him off.

"Just look at all the dog hairs over my sofa," Mrs Trigg complained.

"Sorry, Mrs Trigg," James apologised.

While Mrs Trigg went to get a brush, Mandy cast a quick look round the living-room. The fire burned brightly in the grate, but everything was too neat and tidy to be comfortable and welcoming. There wasn't a Christmas decoration in sight and, worst of all, no Christmas tree.

"I guess we'd better be going," Mandy said to Max.

Max nodded. "I'll see you tomorrow at school," he replied.

"Why don't you come to Animal Ark for tea?" Mandy suggested, as Mrs Trigg came back into the room with a dustpan and brush. "Grandad will walk over to Animal Ark with you; he's coming round anyway. And bring Sandy. Then we can go to carol practice together afterwards."

The carol singers had arranged a practice session at the village hall. Mrs Ponsonby had promised to supervise them, and coach them! Mrs Ponsonby was chairwoman of the Welford Women's Institute. She always liked to get involved in anything that was happening in the village. In fact, she usually reckoned she should be in charge.

"Can I go with Sandy to Mandy's house for tea tomorrow, Gran?" Max asked. "Mandy's grandad will walk me round there."

"Haven't your mum and dad got enough animals to look after, without Sandy getting under their feet?" Mrs Trigg asked Mandy.

Mandy smiled. "Oh, no," she assured Mrs Trigg. "They won't mind at all. They love animals – and they'll adore Sandy. He's so sweet."

Mrs Trigg looked unsure. "I don't know about sweet," she said. "Animals just make a mess as far as I can see."

"But they're such good companions," Mandy went on. "Mrs Ponsonby is always saying how lonely she would be without Pandora." Mrs Ponsonby might be the bossiest woman in Welford, but she really loved Pandora, her Pekinese.

Mrs Trigg looked thoughtful as she bent to brush the dog hairs off the sofa. James nudged Mandy and she followed his eyes. Sandy had crept into the room after Mrs Trigg. He stretched a paw up to the low coffee table where Mrs Trigg's knitting lay, neatly rolled up. Before Max could get to him he had loosened the ball of wool and it had dropped to the floor. Sandy scampered after it just as Mrs Trigg turned round.

"No!" she said sternly to the little dog as he made to pounce on the ball of wool. "Sit!"

Sandy looked up at her, then sat down obediently, his head on one side. As Mrs Trigg bent down to pick up her wool, the little dog lifted his right paw and held it out to her.

Mandy couldn't help smiling; he looked so adorable.

"That's a trick I taught him," Max said proudly. "He wants to shake hands, Gran."

"Hmmph," said Mrs Trigg. Rather stiffly, she quickly "shook hands" with Sandy, then wiped her hand on her apron. "You'd be

better teaching him to do as he's told," she added.

"But he *did*, Mrs Trigg," Mandy put in. "He sat down when you told him, and he hasn't even touched the ball of wool."

Mrs Trigg stood with the dustpan and brush in her hand, looking at Sandy. "I suppose you're right, Mandy," she admitted. "He obviously recognises a firm tone of voice."

James looked out of the window. "Oh, look!" he said. "It's started to snow. We can go sledging at the weekend if it settles."

Mandy and Max rushed to the window. Big fat flakes of snow were falling, swirling in the light from the window.

"Isn't it lovely?" Mandy breathed. "It's so *Christmassy!*"

"But it makes a terrible mess when it melts," Mrs Trigg said.

Mandy looked at the old woman. Her dark navy cardigan was buttoned right up to the neck and the white collar of her blouse was crisp and neat. Her skirt was dark and neat too. Even her apron looked as if it had been starched and pressed. Everything about her was neat and buttoned-up. Her short grey hair was tucked behind her ears – neatly!

"But the snow is beautiful while it lasts, Mrs Trigg," Mandy said. "Don't you think so?"

Mrs Trigg came to stand beside them. She turned her face up to watch the snowflakes falling. "Your grandad used to love snow, Max," she said softly. "You probably don't remember, but when you were a very little boy he made a snowman with you out in the garden, there."

Mandy looked at Mrs Trigg. Her face was softer somehow – as if she was remembering a lot of happy things.

Sandy had scampered up to join them. Max picked him up and looked up at his gran. "I remember," he said. "Grandad made me the best snowman in the world." Mrs Trigg put her arm around her grandson's shoulder and hugged him.

"We'd better go," Mandy said quietly.

"Shall I take Sandy out to the potting

shed then?" Max asked his gran, reluctantly.

Sandy lifted his head and licked Mrs Trigg's hand. The old woman drew her hand away, wiping it on her apron again. But then she said briskly, "Maybe we'd better let him sleep in the warm kitchen tonight."

"Oh thanks, Gran!" Max said, his face lighting up.

Mrs Trigg smiled at her grandson. "But I won't have him in the rest of the house," she warned. "I can't do with all these dog hairs around," she said, giving Blackie a stern look.

Mandy and James grinned at each other. Max was cuddling Sandy as if he would never let him go, and Mrs Trigg was bustling about, sweeping up more invisible dog hairs.

"Come on, Blackie," James said. "Let's go home. See you tomorrow, Max."

The carol singers gathered in the village hall the following afternoon. James and Max had brought Blackie and Sandy, and Peter Foster had turned up with Timmy, his Cairn terrier. The others had left their pets at home until the big day. Mrs Ponsonby couldn't complain about the dogs being there: she had brought Pandora.

"*Hark! the herald-angels sing . . .*" sang the carol singers.

Mrs Ponsonby stood in front of them, waving her arms around. "Louder!" she boomed. "*Glory to the new-born King!*" Her voice wavered on the high notes and Mandy suppressed a giggle. Blackie began to howl as Mrs Ponsonby's voice wobbled through the carol.

"At least Mrs Ponsonby isn't coming out carol singing with us," Gary Roberts said, grinning.

"Don't count on it," Jill Redfern replied.

"*Peace on earth, and mercy mild,*" Mandy sang. She gave Jill a dig in the ribs and Jill joined in.

"*God and sinners reconciled,*" the carollers roared.

Blackie scampered over to where Pandora was sitting behind her owner. The Pekinese was watching the carol singers and joining

in now and again with short, sharp yelps.
Blackie gave Pandora a nudge with his nose
and Pandora yelped even more.

Mrs Ponsonby turned. "Blackie!" she
thundered. The Labrador took off and
streaked under a chair.

James made a dive for Blackie as Mrs
Ponsonby scooped Pandora up and clasped
her pet to her chest.

"Sorry, Mrs Ponsonby," James apologised,
as the carol singing drifted to a stop.

"Really, James," Mrs Ponsonby scolded.
"If you can't keep that dog of yours under

control, you shouldn't bring him to rehearsals. Oh, my poor darling," Mrs Ponsonby murmured to Pandora. "Did wicked Blackie upset you?"

Pandora sneezed, jumped out of Mrs Ponsonby's arms and raced off behind the piano. Sandy scampered after her and Mrs Ponsonby let out a screech.

"Pandora must *not* be overexcited," she declared. "My little angel is so highly strung."

"Whoops!" said Peter Foster as Timmy shot off after the other dogs. Peter made a lunge for his pet but Timmy managed to slip out of his grasp. The dogs had clearly had enough carol singing for the day; they wanted to play. In no time at all they were rolling around and chasing one another.

"Look at them!" said Max, delightedly. "They're having a great time."

"They're leading my precious Pandora astray," Mrs Ponsonby wailed, as she waded into the midst of the dogs, scattering them in all directions. Blackie bumped into a chair and it fell over, spilling song sheets on the floor.

"What a noise!" a voice said from the door. "I thought Mrs Ponsonby was in charge of you all."

Mandy swung round. Mrs Trigg stood there, looking very disapproving. Mandy looked at her watch; it must be time to go. Mrs Trigg had insisted on coming to collect Max. She took the responsibility of looking after him very seriously and always seemed worried in case anything should happen to him while he was in her care.

"I *am* in charge, Maggie," Mrs Ponsonby declared, coming out from behind the piano. Her face was as red as the pompom on her hat. She had been chasing after Pandora. At that moment, Pandora scampered up to her and Mrs Ponsonby bent down and picked up her pet. Carol sheets were scattered on the floor and several more chairs had been overturned.

Max wrestled a rather chewed sheet of music from Sandy, and handed it back to Mrs Ponsonby. "Sorry, Mrs Ponsonby," he said.

Mrs Ponsonby took the soggy piece of

paper. "Don't worry about it, my dear! We've got plenty." The carollers cheerfully carried on tidying up.

Mrs Trigg looked around and sniffed. "Animals!" she said. "What a mess they cause!"

Sandy gave a short bark and shot across the room to Mrs Trigg, wagging his tail furiously. No matter what Mrs Trigg thought of Sandy, the little dog loved *her*.

"Hmmph!" said Mrs Trigg as Sandy sat down almost on top of her boots and thumped his stumpy tail. "I see *you've* been naughty, too," she said sternly, looking down at the little dog. But Mandy noticed that she bent to give him a quick pat.

Mrs Trigg shook her head at Mrs Ponsonby. "It seems to me that pets are nothing but trouble," she announced.

Mrs Ponsonby drew herself up. "I can't agree with you, Maggie," she declared. "Pandora is very well-behaved – usually. And she is such a good companion to me. I wouldn't be without her for the world. I'm never lonely with my Pandora around."

Pandora settled down in Mrs Ponsonby's arms, rubbing her head against her owner's hand.

Mrs Trigg looked at the little dog. "Well, there *is* that," she agreed. "Sometimes I do get lonely," she added softly.

"Then you really should think about having a pet, Maggie," Mrs Ponsonby said briskly. "You'd never feel alone if you had a little dog like my Pandora to keep you company. Didn't I see you walking Sandy this morning?"

Mrs Trigg flushed. "Max was at school," she explained. "Sandy needed a walk."

"That's another thing about dogs," Mrs Ponsonby continued. "They get you out of the house – you would meet people. You spend far too much time cleaning that cottage of yours, my dear. Why don't you come back to the WI? You used to enjoy it so much and you need to get out more!"

With that, Mrs Ponsonby turned away and began to shepherd the children into their coats and hats.

Mrs Trigg looked after her. "Well, really!"

she said, her face rather red.

Mandy came to stand beside Mrs Trigg. "Mrs Ponsonby bosses *everybody* around," she said sympathetically. "But she's right about one thing, Mrs Trigg. Pets can be wonderful company."

"Hmmph!" said Mrs Trigg. "They can also be a lot of hard work. Come along, Max."

Mandy watched as Mrs Trigg bustled Max and Sandy out of the door. Mrs Trigg might have taken Sandy for a walk, but that didn't mean she liked dogs. It wasn't going to be easy changing Mrs Trigg's mind about pets!

# 4

# *An abandoned puppy*

"I think it's going to snow again," Mr Hope said on Saturday morning, as he came into the residential unit at Animal Ark. It had snowed a lot in the last few days. The snow lay deep and thick on the moors around Welford and there were drifts piled high against the hedges in some of the lanes. Even the village green was totally white, and the branches of the surrounding trees were covered in snow.

It was so cold, Mandy had found icicles hanging outside her bedroom window that morning. She had hurried downstairs to put out fresh nuts and bacon rind for the birds; it wasn't easy for them to find food with this much snow around. There would certainly be enough snow for sledging, as long as there wasn't a sudden thaw.

"I hope it snows all day and all night," she said happily. "We're planning to go sledging tomorrow." She had a tiny kitten in her arms. It had swallowed a plastic bottle top, which had lodged in the young animal's throat. Mr Hope had needed to put the kitten to sleep before he could remove it.

"I love sledging," said James, who had arrived after breakfast. "When is Max coming over, Mandy?"

Mandy put the kitten back in its cage. "Any time now," she replied, tickling the little animal under its chin. "He's coming to help choose the Christmas tree. Since he can't have one at Holly Cottage, I thought

he could help decorate ours." It was now
the Christmas holidays – time to put up the
Animal Ark Christmas tree!

"I saw Max's gran out walking Sandy
again yesterday," Mr Hope said. "She
seemed to be getting on really well with
him – much better than she was earlier in
the week."

Mandy smiled. "She's been taking him for
walks while Max has been at school," she
told her father. "She won't have to do that
over the Christmas holidays, of course."

Adam Hope put his head on one side,

looking thoughtful. "Mmm," he said. "Pity. She looked as if she was quite enjoying it."

"Mrs Ponsonby told her she should get a dog," Mandy said.

Mr Hope laughed. "It isn't often you and Mrs Ponsonby agree on anything!"

"Oh, but I think *everybody* should have animals in their life," Mandy declared. "Just look at Max and Sandy."

Max and Sandy had been regular visitors to Animal Ark over the last few days. Max loved seeing the animals and Sandy had made firm friends with Blackie.

"We should get this little fellow home in time for Christmas," Adam Hope remarked, looking at the kitten.

Mandy bent down and smiled at the kitten. "No more bottle tops," she warned. She glanced round the other cages. Only the gerbil and the hamster remained now; the other animals had all gone back to their owners. Mandy was always glad to see animals get well enough to go home, but she missed them when they left.

"I've rung George Fenton," Mr Hope

went on. "He says you can go and choose a tree any time, and I'll pay for it next time I'm passing."

Mr Fenton was Amy's dad. He owned a sawmill just on the edge of the village, and at Christmas he turned his workshop into a Christmas-tree shop.

"Can I choose a really big one, Dad?" Mandy asked.

Emily Hope, Mandy's mum, came through the door just as Mandy was speaking. "Just make sure it'll fit in the living-room," she said, her green eyes twinkling. "We don't want to have to chop the top off."

"I've measured it," Mandy replied. "We can get a two-metre one and still have room to put the star on top!"

"Wow!" said Mrs Hope. "It's just as well you've got Paddy to help bring that home."

Mandy grinned. "We're going to take my sledge," she told her mother. "Paul has been practising with Paddy. He says his pony just loves pulling a sledge – and he's very strong."

"There's Max!" James called, looking out

45

of the window. "Let's go, Mandy."

Mandy glanced outside. The garden was already carpeted in fresh snow. The snowman that she, James and Max had made yesterday stood in the middle of the lawn. There was a covering of snow on the carrot they had used for a nose.

"Wrap up warmly," Mrs Hope called after them as they raced out of the residential unit.

Mandy and James shrugged themselves into heavy jackets, crammed woolly hats on their heads, and thrust their hands into gloves. Blackie rushed out from behind the reception desk to meet them.

"Thanks for looking after him," James said to Jean Knox, the receptionist. Blackie wasn't allowed into the residential unit with the sick animals.

Jean looked over her spectacles at James. "Any time, James," she replied. "He's good company."

Mandy put her head on one side. "I wish Mrs Trigg thought dogs were good company," she said.

"Oh, knowing you, Mandy, you'll persuade her." Jean laughed, nodding her head. Her glasses slid off her nose and bounced on the end of their chain.

"Maybe I will," Mandy said thoughtfully. "You know, she's still letting Sandy sleep in the kitchen because it's been snowing so much. She says she can mop the floor every day."

"That's a lot better than the potting shed for Sandy," Jean agreed.

Mandy opened the door and Sandy threw himself at her. She bent down to let him lick her face in welcome. Blackie bounded out of the door, and the two dogs rolled on the ground, chasing each other and kicking up great flurries of soft, powdery snow.

"Christmas-tree time!" Max said happily.

Mandy smiled. She was *really* glad she had suggested that Max help choose the tree. He seemed so excited about decorating it.

"Here, Blackie," she called, clipping on Blackie's lead as the Labrador bounded up to her.

"I've got the sledge," James called, dragging a red sledge out of the porch. "Let's go!"

First they had to go and collect Paul and Paddy from Paul's house. They roped the sledge to the harness they had rigged up for Paddy. Blackie gave a short bark and leaped on to the sledge. Sandy followed, jumping on behind the Labrador.

Paul grinned as James tried to shoo the dogs off. "Leave them," he said. "It's good practice for Paddy."

As they walked down the main street they made quite a picture. Mr and Mrs McFarlane came out of the post office to watch.

"Are you playing Santa Claus?" Mr McFarlane called to them.

"Paddy makes a good Rudolph, but where's his red nose?" Mrs McFarlane joked.

They laughed and waved. As they passed the Fox and Goose, the landlord, Mr Hardy, came out to watch. "You need some jingle bells," he remarked, smiling.

Mandy looked at Paddy. The sturdy little Exmoor pony really was enjoying pulling the sledge.

Paul had got Paddy from a rescue sanctuary. The little pony had been very badly treated. The first time Mandy saw him, he had been in such poor condition that he wouldn't even have been able to pull a sledge. Now his coat was a glossy greyish brown and his eyes were clear and bright – not sad, the way they had been when Mandy first saw him at the sanctuary.

As Mandy watched, Paddy's head went

up and he shook his dark-brown mane, his breath cloudy on the frosty air. Paul had done a wonderful job with Paddy — and Paddy had loved Paul right from the start.

Mandy laid a hand on Paddy's warm winter coat. "Good boy, Paddy!" she said softly. "Good boy!"

Soon they were out of the village and heading towards the sawmill.

Mandy saw Amy perched on the gate as they turned into the driveway. She stood up, clutching the gate with one mittened hand and waving to them with the other. The bright yellow bobbles on her woolly hat danced merrily as she called out to them. "I've told Dad to show you all the best trees," she told them, swinging the gate open.

Paddy plodded through the gate into the yard and Mr Fenton came out of the shed. "Come on, you lot," he called. "Let's go and choose your tree. Then you can have some mince-pies while I rope it on to the sledge for you."

Mandy and the others followed him excitedly into the shed. The smell of resin and pine needles filled the space. Mandy gazed at the forest of trees propped up against the walls. There were so many to choose from, and each one they looked at seemed better than the last.

Finally, the perfect tree was chosen. "That one!" Max said, pointing to a large, glossy fir tree. The branches of the tree he had selected were feathery and full. Best of all, it had a long, straight top branch.

"Perfect for the Christmas star," Mandy said, smiling happily.

James and Paul nodded in agreement.

"Good choice, Max," James said as he waved to Mr Fenton.

Mandy looked at Max's shining face. He might not have a tree at Holly Cottage, but choosing the one for Animal Ark was surely the next best thing!

"Amy's mum's mince-pies were great," James said as they slowly made their way back down the lane towards Animal Ark.

Mandy laughed. "She promised to have some more ready for us when we go carol singing," she said.

Paul was leading Paddy, guiding the pony carefully over the rough track. Mandy looked up as a large snowflake settled on her nose. "Dad was right!" she exclaimed. "He said it would snow again."

"I wonder if the pool at the bottom of Beacon Hill will be frozen," James said.

"Where's that?" asked Max.

Mandy pointed across the fields to a snow-topped hill. "Over there," she said. "It's a great hill for sledging, and sometimes, if it's really cold, the pool at the bottom freezes over and we can skate on it."

"You have to be careful, though," Paul warned. "The pool is part of the river and the ice has to be really, *really* solid before you try skating."

"Sledging will be enough for me," Max said happily. "You know, Welford is a really great place. We've got a park near where I live, but nothing like this. It must be great living in the country all the time."

Mandy smiled and lifted her face to the snowflakes. "It is," she agreed. "I can't imagine living anywhere else but Welford."

Paddy's hooves were beginning to make marks in the newly fallen snow, and the sledge ran smoothly over the snowy ground. The tree, securely roped on, brushed its branches against Mandy's legs as she walked and the two dogs started chasing snowflakes. If the snow kept up, it was going to be a perfect Christmas.

They turned out of the track on to the back road that ran between the Fentons' sawmill and Welford. Suddenly Sandy stopped at the edge of the ditch that bordered the road. Hanging over the ditch was a bushy bramble, heavy with snow.

"Watch the bramble doesn't prick you, Sandy," Max warned.

Sandy turned his head towards his young master but wouldn't come away from the ditch. He stood there, legs stiff, tail erect, sniffing and growling softly.

"Come on, Sandy," Max said.

But the little dog stayed where he was,

and began to bark urgently.

Max frowned. "What is it, boy?" he asked.

Sandy looked up at him, still barking.

Max gazed down into the ditch. Then he reached out a gloved hand and moved a branch aside. "Oh, no!" he cried out. "Come and look at this."

Mandy hurried over, alerted by the note of shock in Max's voice. "What is it?" she asked. Then she saw for herself, and her heart began to beat faster.

There, lying huddled in the ditch beneath the bramble-bush, was a little puppy. Its coat was dark, but it was fast being covered with snow. And it wasn't moving.

Mandy felt her breath come back in a rush. Then she scrambled down into the ditch and lifted the puppy carefully. She breathed a sigh of relief as, through her gloves, she felt some warmth coming from the puppy's small body. It was alive.

But then Mandy caught sight of the snow where the puppy had lain. She gasped. It was red with blood. There was more blood on her gloves.

She called to the others. "It's a puppy. It's alive – but it's hurt. Bleeding. We've got to get it to Animal Ark as quickly as possible!"

James reached down and took the puppy gently from her. Mandy scrambled out of the ditch, unwrapping her scarf from her neck. "Here," she said. "Wrap this round it. We've got to keep it warm. The poor little thing looks as if it's been there a long time. It's unconscious."

As Mandy muffled the puppy up in her scarf, the little animal opened its eyes and let out a weak cry.

"Oh, the poor little thing," Max said. "It must be in real pain."

Mandy nodded. "The sooner we get back to Animal Ark, the better."

# 5

# *Safe at Animal Ark*

Mandy gazed anxiously at the little puppy as it lay on the examination table at Animal Ark. "How is it?" she asked her mother.

Emily Hope smiled as she finished cleaning the wound on the puppy's leg. "It's a *she*," she said. "I think she's going to be all right. She looks worse than she is, with the fur shaved off around her wound, but it will soon grow back. She's in shock and badly bruised, too, but you got to her just in time, Mandy. Another fifteen minutes in that ditch and she would have died from the cold."

"It was Sandy that found her," Mandy told her mother.

Mrs Hope looked at Max's worried face as he stood on the other side of the examination table. "Then Sandy is a very clever puppy," she said. "Let's go and congratulate him."

Mrs Hope settled the injured puppy comfortably in one of the cages in the residential unit, with a warm blanket tucked round her. "There," she said. "A good sleep and she'll be as right as rain — except for her leg. We'll have to keep an eye on that."

"She won't be lame, will she?" James asked.

Emily Hope shook her head. "It isn't as bad as that," she assured him. "She should be ready to leave us in a few days."

"But she hasn't got a home," Mandy said. "She doesn't even have a collar. And she's so tiny. How old is she, Mum?"

"About five months," Mrs Hope replied. "I'll be able to examine her better tomorrow, but I'd say she's probably had all her injections."

"How do you think she got into the ditch, Mrs Hope?" James asked.

Mandy's mum looked serious. "I think she was abandoned," she said. "It happens sometimes. People get a puppy and forget that they are a lot of work. Then they take them out into the country and just let them go."

"But she was *hurt*," Mandy protested.

Mrs Hope looked sympathetically at Mandy. "Sometimes people just throw the pup out of a moving car," she explained. "It's a terrible thing to do, but at least this little puppy has been saved – thanks to you lot."

Mandy shook her head. *How could anyone be so cruel?* "Oh, I promised I'd phone Paul," she said. "He had to take Paddy home and he's really worried about the puppy."

"You do that," Mrs Hope said. "Then we can cheer ourselves up by decorating the Christmas tree."

Max's face lit up. "Can I stay and help?" he asked.

Mandy turned to him as they went out of the door. "Of course you can," she declared. "You're the chief tree decorator this year!"

Blackie and Sandy bounded over to them as they went into the reception area. Max grinned and bent down to give Sandy a cuddle. "And you're a hero, Sandy," he said.

Blackie gave a short bark. "See," said James. "Blackie thinks so as well."

"I wonder if Holly will like the tree," Max said.

"Holly?" asked Mrs Hope.

Max blushed. "Oh, that's what I was calling the puppy we rescued – just to myself. It's sort of Christmassy, don't you think?"

"I think Holly's a great name," Mandy agreed, when she came back from making her phone call to Paul. She turned to her mother. "What will happen to her?" she asked.

"She'll have to go to the RSPCA once she's better," Mrs Hope replied. "It should only be a few days – Christmas Eve at the latest."

Mandy frowned. "But then nobody would be able to adopt her until after Christmas, Mum," she said. "You know how many puppies are abandoned then. It will be really hard for them to find her a home."

Emily Hope sighed. "I know," she said. "But what else can we do? I can't send her to the RSPCA until her leg is better. They have such a lot of work already and, besides, they wouldn't allow anyone to adopt her until her leg had healed."

Mandy raised her head. "*We* could find her a home," she said. "We could find somebody here in Welford to take her."

Mrs Hope laughed. "I wouldn't put it past you, Mandy," she said. "Now, how about putting up that Christmas tree before Holly wakes up?"

Mandy, James and Max quickly set to work covering the tub for the tree with some bright Christmas paper.

Mr Hope arrived just as they finished. He had been out visiting one of the local farms and his beard was dusted with snow. "It's snowing again," he said, moving towards the fire. "It's freezing out there."

"Do you think it's cold enough for the pool at the bottom of Beacon Hill to ice over?" James asked.

"I should imagine so," Adam Hope replied.

But Mandy wasn't thinking of ice-skating.

She plunged straight into their story about Holly, dragging her father into the residential unit to see the puppy. Adam Hope bent down to look at the sleeping pup. Holly was curled up, cosy and warm in her blanket. She was fast asleep, her nose twitching. Now and again she made soft snuffling noises.

"What breed is she, Dad?" Mandy whispered.

"She looks like some sort of terrier-cross to me," Mr Hope replied. "A pretty little thing," he added, smiling. "Terriers — especially cross-breeds — are tough little things. No wonder Holly survived her ordeal."

"Well, she's safe now," Mandy breathed. "With people who will be kind to her," she added.

Adam Hope ruffled his daughter's hair. "Come on," he said. "Let's leave her to sleep. We can bring her out later to see the Christmas tree."

"Oh, isn't it beautiful!" Mandy exclaimed,

gazing at the Christmas tree. The dark-green branches shimmered in the firelight, giving out a wonderful scent in the heat of the room.

"It'll look even more beautiful when it's decorated," Mrs Hope said, coming into the room with a huge cardboard box in her hands. Blackie and Sandy followed at her heels. The dogs had been banned from the living-room while Mr Hope was putting up the tree. Now they stopped, side by side, and looked at the tree, sniffing the fircones. Sandy launched himself at the tree and Max made a leap for him.

"Leave him," said Mr Hope.

Max drew back, puzzled. Sandy rushed at the tree. As the prickly branches caught his nose, he jumped back, his head low. Cautiously he moved forward again, testing the needles on the branches. Then he sneezed.

"I think he'll keep his distance now." Mrs Hope laughed.

Max laughed too. "This is Sandy's first Christmas," he said.

"So let's make it a really good one," Mandy announced, rummaging in the decorations box. "Look! I've found the star for the top of the tree!"

Half an hour later, Mr Hope moved the stepladder away from the tree. Outside, the afternoon had grown dark. The light from the log fire lit up the glittering baubles of glass, the sparkly tinsel and the gold-wrapped candy sticks hanging from the tree's branches. Mr Hope plugged in the fairy lights. "Who's going to switch them on, then?" he asked.

Mandy spun round, a wide smile on her lips. "Max," she said.

Max walked slowly over to the switch and pressed it down. The tiny white bulbs sprang into life, dancing on the shiny decorations and glowing against the darkness outside.

"Wow!" said James. "That is just the *best* tree ever!"

Sandy and Blackie crept closer to the tree, lying down under it and gazing up at the twinkling lights.

"Now it *really* feels like Christmas,"

Mandy said, smiling happily.

"And I smell mince-pies," James added.

Everybody laughed. "Trust James!" said Mrs Hope. "Come on, you lot; you deserve a treat after all your hard work. Mince-pies all round."

# 6

# *Sandy in danger*

"Holly is looking much better today," Mrs Hope told Mandy next day as she examined the little pup.

"Isn't she beautiful?" Mandy said, as Holly looked up at Mrs Hope and gave her hand a trusting lick. The puppy's little face looked adorable. "Why on earth would anyone abandon her? She's perfect."

"Who knows?" said her mother. "The important thing is that she's a fine, healthy pup and her leg will soon be better."

"When do you think her bandage can come off, Mum?" Mandy asked.

"Tomorrow," Mrs Hope told her. "The wound wasn't very deep and it's healing nicely."

"But we don't have to send her away yet, do we?" Mandy asked.

Mrs Hope shook her head. "I'd like to keep her for a few more days, just to make sure she isn't suffering from delayed shock. She's still very young and she must have had quite a fright."

Mandy frowned. "But it'll be Christmas in three days' time," she said.

"Don't worry," Mrs Hope said. "We won't put her out in the snow."

Mandy smiled. "Oh, I know *that*, Mum," she said. She looked out of the window. "James and Max and I are going sledging on Beacon Hill this morning."

Mrs Hope rose from the table. "I wish I

could come with you. It's years since I've been sledging."

"Why don't you?" Mandy asked.

Mrs Hope smiled. "Because I've got patients to see," she said. "Now, remember: wrap up—"

"Warmly," Mandy finished, grinning. "We will."

"Shh!" said Max to Mandy and James when they arrived at Holly Cottage. He was smiling.

"What is it?" whispered James.

Max put a finger to his lips and led them towards the living-room door. It was open slightly and Mandy and James peered into the room. Mrs Trigg was sitting on the sofa in front of the fire, dozing – and beside her, curled up at her side, was Sandy.

"What is she going to say when she wakes up?" Mandy whispered, grinning.

Max shook his head. "Gran said Sandy could come into the living-room because the weather was so cold," he explained.

"So she's getting to like him?" James asked.

"She won't admit it," Max said. "But I think she is. Only I don't know what she's going to say if she wakes and finds that Sandy has crept up to sit beside her – on the sofa!"

Just at that moment a log shifted in the fire and Mrs Trigg stirred. Her hand went out and touched Sandy's neck. Sandy lifted his head and licked her hand.

Mrs Trigg's eyes flew open and she looked down at the little dog. "Well, really, Sandy!" she said sternly. "Get down at once."

Sandy looked up at her and snuggled closer, clearly delighted at having sneaked up beside Mrs Trigg. Mandy watched in amazement as the old lady's mouth curved in a reluctant smile.

"Bad dog," Mrs Trigg said. But this time she didn't say it as if she meant it. She stood up and brushed her hands down her apron. "Look what you've done, Sandy," she scolded. "Now I've got dog hairs on my apron."

Sandy jumped down off the sofa and wagged his tail, then he rubbed his head against Mrs Trigg's ankles and nibbled at her shoe laces.

"Silly little dog," Mrs Trigg said, bending down and giving him a pat. "Shoo! I've got work to do."

Mandy, James and Max looked at one another. Maybe Sandy was winning Mrs Trigg round after all!

The sun was shining on the crisp, white snow as Mandy, James and Max made their way to Beacon Hill. Mandy looked at the pool at the foot of the hill. "We could try skating another day," she said. "The ice looks firm enough."

Blackie gave a short bark and raced on ahead towards the pool.

Sandy followed, overtaking Blackie and rolling in the snow in front of him. The two dogs leaped and rolled together. They were having a great time.

"They love playing together, don't they?" Max said.

James smiled. "The best of friends," he agreed as Blackie dived into a snowdrift and started kicking up enormous clouds of snow.

Sandy scampered out of range, waiting for his chum to reappear out of the snowdrift. As Mandy watched, she saw Sandy go very still and turn towards the pool, as if he had just heard something.

Mandy looked across the shining sheet of ice but couldn't see anything. "What's Sandy doing?" she asked Max.

Max shrugged. "Maybe he heard a bird or a rabbit," he said.

Mandy nodded. "Oh, look at Blackie!" She giggled.

Blackie burst out of the snowdrift, shaking snow in great dollops from his coat.

"It's a snowstorm!" James yelled.

Blackie barked and began to race past Sandy, towards the frozen pool beyond.

As Blackie ran towards the pool, Sandy turned and gave chase, running at Blackie and growling. The Labrador steered clear of him, keeping away from the pool.

Max frowned. "What on earth is Sandy doing?" he asked. "He's never done that before!"

Blackie ran towards the terrier again, trying to get round him, but Sandy stood his ground, his teeth bared.

"Sandy!" Max called. "Stop that!"

James ran ahead and grasped Blackie's collar. At once Sandy relaxed, coming to Max and wagging his tail.

"What was all that about?" Max asked, puzzled. "They usually get on so well together."

James shrugged. "Sandy seems all right

now," he said. "Come on, let's go sledging."

They trudged up to the top of the hill.

"Race you to the bottom!" James yelled, pushing his sledge off from the top of Beacon Hill.

"That's not fair – you've got a head start," Mandy called after him as she pushed her own sledge off.

The snow was deep and soft. Mandy's sledge skimmed over it, sending up flurries of powdery snow as she went. The sky was a clear blue and, below, the frozen pool was silver in the winter sun.

"Wait for me," called Max, behind her.

Mandy turned to watch as Max launched himself down the slope. When she turned back she shouted, "James! Get out of the way!"

James, in front of her, turned round briefly as Mandy's sledge shot down the hill. But he was too late; Mandy was going to crash into him. James turned his sledge wildly, trying to get out of her path. Blackie bounded past downhill with Sandy at his heels. The dogs were having a wonderful time.

"Uh-oh!" Mandy said, dragging on the ropes of her sledge as she hurtled towards James.

Max took a wide sweep to avoid them both. "See you at the bottom," he called, as Mandy's sledge crashed into James's. The two sledges overturned, tipping Mandy and James out into the snow. Mandy sat up, laughing, as James dived head first into a snowdrift.

"Are you all right?" she spluttered.

James's head appeared, covered in snow. He clambered back on to his sledge. "I'll *still* race you!" he said.

But Mandy wasn't listening. Down near the pool at the bottom of the hill Sandy was barking furiously. "Look!" Mandy exclaimed. "Sandy is acting oddly again."

As Max's sledge made its way downhill, the little dog ran up to meet it, running right in its path. Max turned his sledge, desperately trying to avoid Sandy. For a few moments his sledge ran along the side of the hill and Sandy slowed down.

Max steered his sledge downwards again.

But again Sandy ran in front of him, barking furiously.

The ice on the pool gleamed in the sunshine. As they watched, Max once more turned his sledge sharply to avoid Sandy. This time the sledge overturned and he fell out on to the snow. But Sandy was going too fast to stop. The little dog skidded on the edge of the ice and shot out on to the surface of the pool, scrabbling widely to keep his balance.

"On, no!" Mandy cried. "Look, James!" The ice beneath Sandy was beginning to crack up.

Sandy scrabbled desperately for a footing on the slippery surface. Max got up and began to race towards his pet.

"No, Max! Wait!" James yelled. "The ice is cracking!"

Mandy and James pushed their sledges off, racing downhill. Mandy got there first and grabbed Max. "You can't go out there," she gasped. "The ice won't take your weight. We could see cracks all over the pool from further up the hill."

Max's face was white. "But what about Sandy?" he asked. "If the ice gives way, he'll drown!"

# 7

# *Rescue!*

"What are we going to do?" James asked. Blackie strained forwards; he wanted to help Sandy. James kept a tight hold on his collar.

Mandy frowned, thinking hard. Then an idea came to her. "We've got the sledges," she said. "We can lay one of them down at the edge of the ice where it's thickest. It would be like a platform. And the sledges are plastic; they aren't heavy."

"I think mine is even lighter than yours, Mandy," James said.

"That's it then," said Max. "If you two hold on to the sledge, I can crawl out and try to reach Sandy."

"You?" Mandy sounded surprised.

Max looked at her seriously. "Sandy *is* my dog," he said.

Mandy glanced quickly at the puppy out on the ice. He was about two metres from the bank; cracks were spreading out around him. There was no time to lose and no time to argue.

"Right," she said. "You go on, Max. We'll pull the sledge in if the ice cracks under you."

"Stay, Blackie!" James ordered.

The Labrador looked up at him worriedly, but didn't move even when James let go of his collar.

Quickly, Mandy and James laid James's sledge down on the ice at the edge of the pool and Max began to crawl along the makeshift platform. The ice groaned under

him and Mandy held her breath, watching
the boy edge out towards his pet. She and
James hung on tightly to the end of the
sledge. There was a sudden snap as a large
piece of ice further out broke loose and
turned on its side. It floated for a moment
before breaking up.

"That water will be really cold," James
said worriedly.

Mandy nodded and bent down, ready to
pull in the sledge if necessary.

Max looked back. "I don't know if I can
reach him," he said.

Mandy watched while Max inched his way along the sledge as far as he could go. He was as close to Sandy as he could get now.

Sandy was gazing at Max, but Max couldn't reach him. Even with his arms outstretched, Sandy was still about twenty centimetres away from Max. Max stretched out a hand. "Come on, Sandy," he coaxed. "Jump for it. Jump on to the sledge."

There was another groan and then a loud crack. Mandy saw the ice under Sandy crack right across. Sandy's paws scrabbled at the ice under him as it split from side to side, leaving a great, gaping hole. Then he lost his balance, tumbling into the water. Max made a lunge and the breath stopped in Mandy's throat as the sledge wobbled on the very edge of the ice hole.

"Max!" she yelled.

But Max wasn't listening; Sandy had disappeared beneath the water. There was a flurry and the little dog appeared, struggling to stay afloat.

Blackie made to rush forward on to the

ice but James caught his collar. "No, boy," he said. "I know you want to help, but we can't have two of you out there."

"Don't let him sink under the ice," Mandy muttered, her eyes on Sandy. "He'd be trapped. Swim, Sandy, swim!"

As if he heard her, Sandy started to doggy-paddle towards Max. Another raft of ice floated towards him, grazing his side, pushing him further away from Max and forcing him underwater.

Max made a final grab, plunging his hand into the water as Sandy disappeared again. Then, with a heave, Max pulled Sandy free and hauled him up on to the sledge. At once, James and Mandy gently started to pull the sledge back until it rested at the edge of the pool. Max clambered off with Sandy in his arms.

"You did it, Max," James said.

But Max's expression was worried. "He's so cold. We'll have to get him back as quickly as we can."

Mandy unzipped her anorak. "Yours is wet, Max," she explained. "But mine is dry.

Sandy will be warm tucked up in here."

Max put Sandy gently into Mandy's arms and she zipped her fleecy anorak up around him. "There," she said to the shivering little dog. "Now we have to get you back to Animal Ark as quickly as possible."

Mr Hope was in the surgery when they arrived. Jean Knox rang through to him at once, then she bundled the children and dogs into the warmth of the living-room. A fire blazed cheerfully in the grate and the Christmas tree lights were on, but Mandy was too worried to admire them.

They laid Sandy down in front of the fire. The little animal was still shaking with cold, but not quite as much as he had been. Jean brought two big fluffy towels – one for Sandy and one for Max.

"Get that wet anorak off," she said to Max. "You're shivering. Mandy can rub Sandy down while I get her a dry jumper."

Mandy wrapped one of the towels round the little dog, rubbing the warmth back into him, while Max took off his anorak.

Underneath, his jumper was also wet.

"I'll get you one of Mandy's," Jean said briskly, going out of the door. "And I've phoned your gran. She's coming right over."

Mandy finished rubbing Sandy down and changed into a dry jumper. The one she had been wearing was wet all down the front where Sandy had snuggled close to her. Blackie curled up beside Sandy.

"Good boy, Blackie," she murmured to the Labrador. "You're helping to keep him warm too."

Max dried himself off and slipped on the jumper that Jean brought for him.

"Your dad is just coming," Jean said to Mandy. "What on earth happened?"

At that moment Mr Hope came in, and Mandy explained while her father examined the puppy.

"Well," he said, standing up. "The little fellow seems none the worse for his adventure. You three seem to be turning into a Welford Dog Rescue Team. That's the second pup you've rescued in the last few days!" He looked serious suddenly. "But, you know, that was a very dangerous thing to do, Max."

"It certainly was," added a voice from the door.

Mandy looked round. Mrs Trigg was standing there in her black coat and hat. Her face was white with worry and she looked angry. "What on earth were you thinking of, Max? You might have been drowned – and all for the sake of that dog. I might have known – animals are nothing but trouble! He'll have to go!" she declared.

Mandy's heart sank. Mrs Trigg had been growing fond of Sandy, she was sure of it. Now she seemed to hate him more than ever.

Max looked dumbly at his grandmother, the tears standing in his eyes. Mandy felt suddenly angry. It was so unfair! She could understand how worried and upset Mrs Trigg was, but she had got it all wrong.

"That isn't true, Mrs Trigg," she burst out. "Sandy was trying to *help* Max."

Mrs Trigg looked down her nose at

Mandy. "Help?" she said. "You call getting itself half drowned and putting Max in danger *helping*?"

"No," said Mandy. "You don't understand. Sandy knew the ice was thin; James and Max will tell you." She turned to the boys. "Remember how Sandy warned Blackie off the ice? He growled and bared his teeth."

"That's right," agreed James. "He had never behaved like that before. We wondered what was wrong."

"Nonsense," Mrs Trigg said.

"Maybe not, Mrs Trigg," Mr Hope cut in. "Dogs have a very keen sense of hearing. If Sandy had heard the ice creaking and beginning to break up, he might have known instinctively that there was danger out there. Go on, Mandy; tell us exactly what Sandy did."

Mandy took a deep breath. "When Max came downhill on his sledge he was heading towards the pool," she explained. "Sandy kept running in front of him, trying to make him change course. Max lost control of his sledge and it tipped over and he fell out, but Sandy couldn't stop so he ended up out on the ice. If it hadn't been for Sandy, *Max* would have slid right out on to the ice."

She turned to Mrs Trigg, looking pleadingly up at her. "So you see, Mrs Trigg, Sandy saved Max's life. You can't send him away. Anybody can see how much Sandy loves Max, and Max loves Sandy just as much! Max is missing his mum and dad such a lot, and Sandy is his friend. You *can't* take him away from Max – especially not at Christmas time!"

Mandy stopped, afraid she had gone too far. Mrs Trigg looked at her for a long moment. Then the old lady looked away, her eyes going round the room. She gazed at the shining Christmas tree in the window, then her eyes rested on Max and Sandy. Max was sitting in front of the fire with Sandy in his arms. The firelight cast a rosy glow over both of them.

"They certainly seem to love each other," Mrs Trigg said softly to Mandy. She smiled and went on in a low voice, "It's so

Christmassy in here. I remember when my husband was alive we used to have such good Christmases. Oh, how he loved it. He would decorate the cottage from top to bottom and I would bake a Christmas cake – and mince-pies, and brandy-snaps and Yule logs. Oh, everything! I haven't bothered about Christmas much since Bill died. Max's mum and dad haven't been able to come for Christmas in recent years, so it hasn't seemed worth it just for myself."

"But it *isn't* just yourself this year, Mrs Trigg," Mandy said gently.

Mrs Trigg looked at her in surprise. "You know, you're right, Mandy," she said. "My cottage isn't very Christmassy. Maybe I should do something about that, my dear."

Mandy smiled at the old lady. She wasn't angry after all.

Then Mrs Trigg spoke briskly. "Let's get you home, Max," she said. "Sandy, too. It seems that I owe him an apology. Perhaps he could sit with us in the living-room from now on — but not on the furniture."

Max's face lit up. "Can he lie on the rug in front of the fire? He's had such a shock today. He nearly drowned."

"I think that would be all right," said his grandmother. "Come along now."

"Can I go and see Holly first?" Max asked.

"Holly?" said Mrs Trigg.

Max nodded. "It's a puppy that Sandy found," he explained. "The poor little thing was abandoned. She would have frozen to death if it hadn't been for Sandy."

Mrs Trigg smiled. "It seems I've got a lot to learn about Sandy," she said.

"Would *you* like to see Holly, Mrs Trigg?" Mandy asked.

Mrs Trigg looked surprised. "Me?" she said. "Why would I want to see a puppy?"

Mandy smiled. "Oh, you might like her," she suggested, with a grin.

Mrs Trigg looked round the eager faces of the children. "I suppose I might as well have a look," she said after a moment. "After all, what harm can it do?"

Mandy's smile got even wider. "None at all, Mrs Trigg," she said. "None at all."

# 8

# *Mrs Trigg's surprise*

Mrs Trigg followed the others into the residential unit. Mandy unhooked Holly's cage and lifted her out. "How are you?" she whispered, cuddling the little puppy.

Holly looked up at her and licked her nose. Mandy giggled.

"We've brought somebody new to see

you," James said. "Say hello to Mrs Trigg, Holly."

Mandy held the puppy out to the old woman. Mrs Trigg took a step back. "Oh, I don't think I could," she said.

"She's very gentle, Gran," Max assured his grandmother.

Mrs Trigg held out her arms slowly and Mandy put the puppy into them. Holly snuggled down and closed her eyes.

"She'll soon be as good as new," Mandy said.

Mrs Trigg stood quite still, looking at Holly. She was holding the puppy a little awkwardly, but Holly didn't seem to mind. Holly opened her eyes for a moment and nibbled at the old lady's fingers. Mandy tickled the puppy under the chin. "She likes you doing that," she said to Mrs Trigg.

Mrs Trigg put a finger under Holly's chin. The puppy looked up at her with big melting eyes and yawned.

"Isn't she adorable?" Max said.

"What exactly happened to her?" Mrs Trigg asked, looking at Holly's bandage.

Mandy laid her hand lightly on Holly's leg. "Holly was abandoned," she explained. "Mum thinks she was thrown out of a moving car."

Mrs Trigg looked up, her face shocked. "How dreadful," she said. "How could anyone be so cruel?"

"People do that kind of thing all the time," James said sadly. "But at least Holly was saved."

"Holly . . ." Mrs Trigg repeated the name. "That's the name of my cottage."

Mandy nodded. "It was Sandy who found her. She had just been left to die in the snow. She was hurt and really cold when we brought her in. If it hadn't been for Sandy, Holly wouldn't be alive now."

Mrs Trigg looked thoughtful. "It seems that Sandy is quite a clever dog," she remarked.

Mandy nodded. "Oh, he is," she agreed. "And Holly is the sweetest little thing. She has a lovely nature. But she'll have to go to the RSPCA soon."

"And what will happen to her then?"

asked Mrs Trigg, rubbing Holly's ears gently with a finger. Holly snuffled and sneezed. Mrs Trigg laughed.

"They'll try to find a home for her," Mandy explained. "But it's a difficult time of year. Lots of people get puppies at Christmas and then get rid of them when they find out how much work is involved. There are so many abandoned puppies after Christmas that she might not find a home at all."

"And what would happen then?" asked Mrs Trigg.

Mandy laid a hand on Holly's furry head and stroked the puppy's nose. "She would have to be put down," she explained.

Mrs Trigg frowned. "That would be a pity," she said. "Especially after you saved her. She isn't a very young puppy, is she?"

Mandy shook her head. "Holly is about five months old. She's had all her injections and everything – and she's toilet-trained."

Holly nibbled at Mrs Trigg's gloved fingers. "I've never thought pets were very useful," she said thoughtfully.

Mandy rubbed Holly's ears. "They *can* be," she said. "Just think about all the seeing and hearing dogs there are. But the great thing about pets is that they love you and they're good company."

Mrs Trigg looked even more thoughtful. "That's what Amelia Ponsonby said. Holly seems well enough behaved."

"Holly is *gorgeous*," Mandy declared, burying her face in the puppy's soft coat.

"Hmmph!" said Mrs Trigg, suddenly brisk. "Well, I can't stand here all day holding a puppy. It's time Max and I went home."

"And Sandy," added Max.

Mrs Trigg smiled and handed Holly back to Mandy. "And Sandy," she agreed. Mandy and James watched as Mrs Trigg bundled Max out of the unit.

"Do you think there's any chance of us finding a home for Holly before she has to go to the RSPCA?" James asked.

Mandy looked thoughtful. She was still thinking of the way Mrs Trigg had held Holly – and she hadn't even bothered to brush down her coat before she left. "You know, James," she said, "I think we might."

On the day before Christmas Eve Mandy got a surprise telephone call from Mrs Trigg. "Can you and James come round to see me?" the old lady asked.

"But Max is here at Animal Ark," Mandy said. "He and Sandy are saying goodbye to Holly. She has to go to the RSPCA today," she said sadly.

"I know Max is there," Mrs Trigg replied. "And I don't want you to tell him you're coming to see me."

"OK," said Mandy, puzzled. "I'll try to get James alone. He's here, too. We'll both come."

"Make it soon," said Mrs Trigg mysteriously. "I've got a surprise for Max."

Mandy managed to get James alone and told him about the phone call. "But what are we going to say to Max?" James asked.

Mandy thought for a moment. "What if I ask him to do me a special favour and groom Holly before she goes away?"

"That would work," said James. "Holly certainly loves being groomed. She won't let you stop once you've started."

Mandy grinned and went to find Max. As expected, he was more than willing. He didn't even ask her where she was going.

Mandy and James rushed round to Holly Cottage. Mrs Trigg was waiting for them and she opened the door at once. James looked at Blackie.

"Shall I tie him up outside?" he asked.

Mrs Trigg shook her head. "Bring him in. Just don't let him jump on the furniture."

James looked at Mandy as they followed Mrs Trigg into the cottage. Mandy shrugged, then she sniffed. She could smell mince-pies baking – and the scent of pine needles. There was something very odd going on at Holly Cottage.

Mrs Trigg ushered them into the living-room and Mandy gasped. There, in the corner of the room, was the prettiest little Christmas tree Mandy had ever seen. It sat in its own plant pot and its needles were glossy and green. Beside it was a box of fairy lights and tree decorations.

"A Christmas tree!" James exclaimed.

"Do you think Max will like it?" Mrs Trigg asked anxiously. "It isn't very big."

"It's perfect," James assured her.

"Is that the surprise?" Mandy asked. "Max will love it."

"There's another surprise," Mrs Trigg said, her eyes shining. "It's wonderful news. I got a call from Max's dad this morning. He and Max's mum *are* going to be here for Christmas after all! Max's mum is coming out of hospital and his dad has unexpectedly been given leave from his work. They're arriving later today."

"Oh, that's wonderful," James exclaimed. "Max will be so happy."

"But don't tell him," Mrs Trigg warned. "I thought I would have a little surprise party this afternoon to celebrate. It's a long time since I had a Christmas party and *years* since I had a tree. I had forgotten how wonderful a real tree smells."

Mandy smiled with delight, then her face fell.

"What is it, Mandy?" Mrs Trigg asked.

"Well," Mandy explained, "it's just that we're all going carol singing this afternoon. Max was going to come, too."

Mrs Trigg pursed her lips. "Well, that's fine," she said at last. "Why don't you all go carol singing and finish up here? Then we can have a party for all the carol singers – and for Max's mum and dad."

"And keep it as a surprise?" asked James.

Mrs Trigg nodded. "When I saw Animal Ark, I realised how much I'd been missing over these last few years in not making much effort over Christmas. Poor Max; my cottage wasn't very Christmassy for him. I want to make up for that, and a party would make it even more like Christmas."

"But Mrs Trigg," Mandy said slowly, "you don't understand. The carol singers are all bringing their pets."

"Pets?" repeated Mrs Trigg.

Mandy nodded. "You know, their dogs and cats — and Amy Fenton's mouse and Jack Gardiner's rabbit."

"There's even a pony," James put in.

Mrs Trigg frowned and Mandy's heart sank. There was no way she would want all those animals in her cottage.

"Well," said Mrs Trigg at last, "I suppose the pony would have to stay outside."

"You mean you would let all the other animals into your cottage?" Mandy squeaked.

Mrs Trigg looked round her living-room. It was bright and cheerful, and not quite as tidy as usual. There were more Christmas decorations spilling out of a box, which was sitting on a chair, and a pile of presents waiting to be wrapped. "I can always clean it up afterwards," she said. "After all, I like a chance to give the cottage a good clean."

Mandy and James looked at each other and laughed.

"Mrs Trigg," said James, pointing to the box on the chair, "would you like us to help you put those decorations up?"

"That would be wonderful, James," Mrs Trigg replied.

Mandy rolled up her sleeves. "OK, where do you want them?" she asked.

Mrs Trigg spread her arms wide. "*Everywhere*, Mandy!"

# 9

# A home for Holly

Mandy had a lot to think about while she and James helped Mrs Trigg with her decorations. As they left Holly Cottage she grabbed James's arm. "James," she said, "do you think *Mrs Trigg* would take Holly?"

James looked at Mandy in surprise. "Mrs Trigg?" he exclaimed. "I know she really likes Sandy – deep down. But would she really want a puppy of her own?"

"She's changed such a lot," Mandy said thoughtfully. "I can't help thinking of the way she looked at Holly. I'm sure she liked her."

James shoved his glasses up on his nose. "Well, we haven't got much time if we're going to try," he said. "Holly will be leaving Animal Ark pretty soon."

"So, let's go," Mandy said. "We've got to ask Mum and Dad."

"I hope we'll get there in time," Mandy gasped as they rushed up the path and into the surgery. They almost collided with Mandy's gran, who was just coming out of the door.

"What's all the hurry?" Gran asked.

"Gran, has Dad left with Holly yet?" Mandy gasped.

"He's just fetching her now. You'll be in time to say a last goodbye."

"Maybe we won't have to," Mandy said hurriedly. "Oh, Gran, Mrs Trigg is going to have a surprise party for Max. His mum and dad are coming home today and she wants the carol singers to go to Holly Cottage after we finish. She's decorating the cottage and baking and – everything."

"Well, well," said Gran. "I'm glad to hear that. I met her yesterday and she was looking a lot more like her old self." Then Gran paused. "Do you think she could do with a bit of help to get ready for the party?"

"I'm sure she could," Mandy said, smiling. "Gran, you're great!"

"You're not so bad yourself," Gran called after Mandy as she rushed into Animal Ark. "I'll get round there right away."

Mr Hope was lifting Holly out of her cage. Emily Hope was with him and so was Max.

"Dad," Mandy gasped, "can we keep Holly just a little while longer?"

Adam Hope frowned. "But we agreed that she should go to the RSPCA today."

"Maybe we won't have to send her at all," James burst out.

Emily Hope smiled. "Now, slow down," she said. "What's all this about?"

"I think I've found a home for Holly," Mandy explained. "I'm almost sure that Mrs Trigg would take her."

"Gran?" Max cried.

Mandy nodded. "She's so much nicer to Sandy now, Max. You know that. And she really liked Holly when she met her – I know she did."

Mrs Hope looked thoughtful. "You said *almost* sure, Mandy," she said. "Haven't you asked her? It's a big risk to take. You know that after Christmas there will be lots more puppies for the RSPCA to find homes for. At least if she goes today there'll be a small chance that somebody might choose her as a pet before Christmas."

Mandy nodded. "I know that, Mum," she said. "But it isn't a very big chance, and I just think that if Mrs Trigg sees Holly again she'll change her mind about having a pet. And it would mean that Holly could stay in Welford. Please – can I try? Please?"

Mr and Mrs Hope looked at each other. Mandy gazed at the little puppy in her father's arms. She couldn't bear to lose Holly entirely.

"I suppose it's worth a try," Mr Hope said at last. "But you mustn't force Mrs Trigg to take her, Mandy."

"Oh, we wouldn't do that," said James.

Max grinned. "They *couldn't* force Gran," he said. "If she says yes, it's because she really wants Holly."

Mandy laid a hand on Holly's silky coat. Max had groomed the little terrier–cross until she gleamed. "Of course she wants Holly," she declared. "She just doesn't *know* it yet!"

Mrs Hope smiled. "All right then,

Mandy," she said. "But if Mrs Trigg *doesn't* want Holly then she'll have to go tomorrow morning. We can't keep her."

Mandy nodded, her face serious again. "I know that, Mum," she said. "But I'm sure I'm right. I'm just sure of it."

Mandy looked at Max. Now all she had to do was keep him at Animal Ark for the afternoon, so that the party would be a surprise. "Let's do some carol practice," she suggested, nudging James. "Then we can all go out singing from here."

"Good idea," said James, taking the hint. "Come on, Max. Let's get the carol sheets."

Mandy looked at James gratefully as he dragged Max out of the door. "I've got another surprise," she announced to her mum and dad, and launched into explanations about the party.

"*Good King Wenceslas looked out*
    *On the feast of Stephen . . .*"
The carol rang round the village as Mandy and her friends sang as they walked up the snowy main street. Even the animals were

joining in. Duchess miaowed along with the music and Blackie gave a bark. Paddy had tinsel threaded through his bridle and a warm red rug on his back. He whinnied softly. All over the village, people came to their doors to hear the carols.

Mandy was carrying Holly in her arms. Her leg was no longer bandaged, but Mandy wanted to be quite sure the little animal came to no harm. The puppy looked up as a flake of snow settled on her nose. More flakes fell, shining in the light of the lamps the children carried. They only had one more house to go now and, as they approached Holly Cottage, Mandy cuddled Holly closer to her. "Not long now, Holly. You'll soon have a new home, I promise you," she whispered to the puppy.

James opened the gate of Holly Cottage and Jill Redfern started a new carol: "*Ding dong merrily on high . . .*"

They all joined in, the sound floating through the frosty air towards the front door. It opened, flooding the path with light. Mrs Trigg stood there waiting for them.

The children grouped themselves round the door and finished the carol. Max was flushed with pleasure.

Mrs Trigg beamed at them. "That was lovely," she said. "Thank you! Now, come in out of the cold. I've got a surprise for you all."

The children trooped into the house. "Take your shoes off," Mrs Trigg ordered, but she said it with a smile.

Paul tied Paddy to the front porch, making sure the pony was protected from the snow.

Leaving their boots and coats in the hall, the carol singers followed Mrs Trigg through to the living-room. Mandy gasped. The tree twinkled in the corner, the room was festooned with decorations and a fire burned brightly in the hearth. But it wasn't the decorations that made her gasp – it was the table, laden with goodies. Along with plates full of delicious-looking tiny sandwiches and rolls, there were others heaped with mince-pies, gingerbread and little iced cupcakes. A beautifully decorated Christmas cake sat in the middle.

"Gran!" breathed Max.

"I thought you would like a party for your friends," Mrs Trigg told him. "Mandy and James helped me keep it a surprise for you. And Mandy's gran helped with the baking. She even brought round a spare Christmas cake she'd baked, as I didn't have time to bake one. We had great fun decorating it this afternoon!"

"But what about all the *animals*?" Max asked.

Mrs Trigg looked round the little choir. Timmy, Peter Foster's Cairn terrier, bounded up to the table and looked longingly at the goodies. Jack Gardiner's rabbit, Hoppy, poked his head round Jack's arm and waggled his ears, and Amy Fenton's mouse, Minnie, twitched her whiskers.

"Don't worry," said Amy. "I won't let her go. She doesn't like Duchess much." The furry Persian cat stalked over to the table and miaowed.

Mrs Trigg laughed. "Just keep them off the furniture," she said. "There are lots of nice things for the pets, too − in the kitchen."

"What about Paddy?" asked Paul.

"There are carrots and apples," Mrs Trigg told him. "Paddy can share them with Jack's rabbit."

Max was looking as if he couldn't believe his ears. Just then the doorbell rang. Mandy's mum and dad trooped in with Gran and Grandad.

"Now the party can really start," said Mrs Trigg happily. "Come on then – tuck in!"

They didn't need to be told twice. Gran beamed at Mrs Trigg. "I was just saying to Tom that we'll have to get you back on the committee of the Women's Institute, Maggie," she said. "We could do with a good cook like you to help with all our functions."

Mrs Trigg flushed. "Oh, Dorothy, I would really like that," she said, her face lighting up.

Mandy was halfway through a plate of egg sandwiches and mince-pies when Mrs Trigg came over to her. Holly was sitting quietly at Mandy's feet. Mandy bent and fed her a bit of sandwich, then picked the little dog up with one hand, balancing her plate in the other.

"This is the puppy that was abandoned, isn't it?" Mrs Trigg asked.

Mandy nodded innocently. "You'd better say goodbye to her, Mrs Trigg," she said. "I was hoping somebody in Welford would adopt her. She's so sweet. I'll really miss her when she goes. It's such a pity she can't stay here among her friends."

"You'd think *somebody* would want her," Mrs Trigg said. "Just look at her beautiful coat."

"She loves being groomed," Mandy continued, watching Mrs Trigg run her hand through Holly's silky hair.

"She's a lovely little thing," Mrs Trigg said. "I hope she finds a good home." Mandy sighed and deliberately tipped her plate just a little. "Can you take her for a moment, Mrs Trigg?" she asked. "I don't want to spill anything."

Mrs Trigg put out her arms and gathered the little puppy into them. "I'm not very good with animals," she said.

Mandy looked at the old lady cradling the puppy. Holly put her head in the crook of Mrs Trigg's arm and yawned. "Oh, I think you are," Mandy said softly. "Holly likes you."

Mrs Trigg looked down at the puppy wonderingly. "Do you really think so?" she asked.

The doorbell rang again. Mrs Trigg went to answer it. A man and woman came into the room, shaking the snow from their coats.

"Oops, sorry about the mess, Mum," the man said, hugging Mrs Trigg. "We were in a rush to see Max."

"Come in! Come in!" Mrs Trigg welcomed them, her eyes sparkling with happiness. "Max, here's another surprise for you."

"Dad! *Mum!*" Max yelled, flying across the room. "How did you get here, Dad? Are you better now, Mum?"

Max's mum held out her arms and Max hugged her while she explained how she got out of hospital early.

"And I got all my work finished early too,

Max," his father explained, ruffling his son's hair. "Mum and I wanted so much to be with you for Christmas."

Max turned, his arms round both his parents. "What a Christmas present!" he said.

His mum looked around. "Oh, you're having a party," she said, looking surprised.

Max's dad grinned. "Look at all these animals, Mum," he said. "This is great. Max won't want to come home with us after Christmas if he's been having such a good time here!"

Max looked at his gran. "Gran has been great," he said. "She's been really kind to Sandy."

Mrs Trigg blushed. "Oh, I don't know about that, Max," she said. "I wasn't very good with him at first."

"That doesn't matter now," Max said. "Sandy thinks you're great."

Sandy scampered across the room and tried to undo Mrs Trigg's shoe laces. "Down, Sandy," Mrs Trigg said, but she was smiling. "That's his favourite game!" she said.

Sandy sat down and looked up at her, wagging his tail.

"And you've got a dog of your own," Max's mum said, coming over to stand beside her mother-in-law and stroke the puppy in her arms.

"Oh, no . . ." Mrs Trigg began.

"Good for you, Mum," her son said. "I've thought for a long while that you should get a pet to keep you company, and a dog is perfect. What's its name?"

"Holly," said Mrs Trigg, looking confused.

"Just like the cottage," Max's mum said, smiling. She had soft brown hair and blue eyes – like Max.

"But she isn't mine," said Mrs Trigg.

Mandy looked up at her. "She *could* be, though," she said gently.

Mrs Trigg looked down at the puppy in her arms. Holly opened her eyes and gazed adoringly back, then she licked Mrs Trigg's hand.

Mandy waited, holding her breath.

"Do you think she would *like* to stay at

Holly Cottage with me?" Mrs Trigg asked.

"I'm sure she would," Mandy replied. "You'd be rescuing her, Mrs Trigg."

"And she would be such good company," Mrs Trigg answered. "I think I'm going to miss Sandy when he goes."

"I'll bring Sandy to see Holly lots of times," Max promised. "They're good friends."

Mrs Trigg looked around at all the eager faces. "I'd love to have her! What an unexpected Christmas gift!" she said.

"And you've given Holly the best Christmas present as well," Mandy assured her. "A home!" She looked across at her mum and dad; they were both smiling. Adam Hope gave her the thumbs-up sign.

"You've given *me* the best Christmas ever, Gran," said Max. "I've never had such a good party."

Mandy and James looked at each other. "A pets' party," Mandy declared. "The best party possible!"

# LUCY DANIELS

*Animal Ark Pets*

*All Hodder Children's books are available at your local bookshop, or can be ordered direct from the publisher. Just tick the titles you would like and complete the details below. Prices and availability are subject to change without prior notice.*

Please enclose a cheque or postal order made payable to *Bookpoint Ltd*, and send to: Hodder Children's Books, 39 Milton Park, Abingdon, OXON OX14 4TD, UK. Email Address: orders@bookpoint.co.uk

If you would prefer to pay by credit card, our call centre team would be delighted to take your order by telephone. Our direct line *01235 400414* (lines open 9.00 am–6.00 pm Monday to Saturday, 24 hour message answering service). Alternatively you can send a fax on *01235 400454*.

| TITLE | | FIRST NAME | | SURNAME | |
|---|---|---|---|---|---|

| ADDRESS | |
|---|---|
| | |
| | |
| | |
| DAYTIME TEL: | | POST CODE | |

If you would prefer to pay by credit card, please complete:
Please debit my Visa/Access/Diner's Card/American Express (delete as applicable) card no:

| | | | | | | | | | | | | | | | |
|---|---|---|---|---|---|---|---|---|---|---|---|---|---|---|---|

Signature ..................................................... Expiry Date: ..................................

If you would NOT like to receive further information on our products please tick the box.  ❏